Contents

Learn to Make Great Digital Photos for 5 Bucks

Tim Grey

Fair Shake Press, an imprint of Pearson Technology Group, division of Pearson Education

Cover photo courtesy of istockphoto.com. Photographer: Lee Pettet.

Composed in the typeface Cronos MM from Adobe Systems

ISBN 0-321-30361-X

9 8 7 6 5 4 3 2 1

Printed and bound in the United States of America

"Yeah, I'd pay five bucks to learn more about that...."

- *Learn the iPod for 5 Bucks* ISBN 0321287851
- *Learn How to Buy and Sell on eBay for 5 Bucks* ISBN 0321287843
- *Learn the Canon EOS Digital Rebel Camera for 5 Bucks* ISBN 0321287827
- *Learn the Nikon Coolpix Camera for 5 Bucks* ISBN 0321287835
- *Learn How to Make Great Digital Photos for 5 Bucks* ISBN 032130361X
- *Learn the Low-Carb Lifestyle for 5 Bucks* ISBN 0321303601
- *Learn How to Win at Texas Hold 'Em Poker for 5 Bucks* ISBN 0321287819

Look for these terrific little books in all kinds of stores, everywhere. Lots more neat little "books for people who hate reading the manual" are on the way.

Keep checking **www.fairshakepress.com**. We'd love to hear what you'd pay five bucks to learn more about…

FairShake
press

How to read this book

Welcome to a new way of learning about high-tech gadgets. This book is different because it's designed for one thing: to teach you just what you need to know, and nothing more, about how to use your digital camera to take high-quality photos of your family, friends, hobbies, trips, and much more. You're not going to learn about the detailed inner workings of your digital camera, or a bunch of high-end image editing techniques with software you probably can't afford to buy. This just isn't that kind of book. Instead, we cover the basics of what you need to know to start taking great digital photos *right now*.

Obviously, there's a lot to learn about photography—a seemingly endless procession of books have been published on the subject and whole magazines are devoted to it. But where do you start? What is it that you simply must know in order to get going? How can you find the few nuggets that will put you straight on the path to successful picture-taking?

This book is designed to answer those questions, whether you are new to photography entirely or simply new to digital photography. You'll find the book divided into four easily-digested sections. Part 1 covers the features you'll find in most consumer digital cameras, explaining what each feature is designed to do and how you can use it to take great photos. Part 2 explains the variety of shooting modes you are likely to encounter. A mode is simply a group of settings that the camera manufacturer has determined is optimal for certain shooting situations such as sports, landscape, or night photography. Part 3 teaches you how to take high-quality photos in a variety of lighting situations such as in full sunlight or when using a flash. Finally, Part 4 offers a batch of slightly more advanced tips, such as how to make the most interesting compositions or how to make sure your colors are as close to perfect as possible.

So pull your new digital camera out of its bag, find something fun to photograph, and start snapping!

Acknowledgments

I'd like to thank my lovely wife (and best friend), Lisa, for continuing to support me in all my endeavors. She must think I'm crazy for taking on so many projects, and I appreciate her love, support, and patience. Miranda helped with many of the pictures in this book, and I enjoyed the time we spent together on the project. Riley is full of endless smiles and gets cuter with every picture. She's an absolute joy.

I'd also like to thank my good friend Bruce Heller for his ongoing support and encouragement. Peter Burian, an excellent photographer and author, is a friend who helped me focus my writing career. Jeff Greene is also a good friend who continues to provide an ear for listening and inspiration with his attention to detail and excellent photography.

Writing about digital photography also means working with the latest digital cameras, and I'd like to extend my sincere thanks to Dave Metz at Canon USA for continuing to be incredibly supportive, and providing me with the opportunity to try out the latest digital cameras from Canon.

Introduction

The first consumer digital camera was released in 1994—ten years ago—and the quality and capabilities have improved dramatically every year since. In the last few years, digital cameras have gotten to the point that they are able to provide excellent quality that can meet or exceed what was possible with film.

With the meteoric rise of digital photography, it seems just about everyone is making the switch to a digital camera. Of course, a new device using new technology also requires new knowledge to use effectively. For those who don't aspire to be professional photographers but simply want to put a digital camera to use recording cherished moments with family and friends, the learning curve can be a source of frustration. For these photographers, many of the books provide too much information, overwhelming readers who just want to learn how to easily take great pictures with their new digital cameras.

This book doesn't attempt to teach you everything there is to know about digital cameras. Instead, it focuses on a narrow range of "must know" information to help you get comfortable right away with your digital camera.

I hope this book will provide a quick and easy way for you to get started taking great pictures with your digital camera, so you can take advantage of the benefits of digital photography while recording those special moments in life.

> *Part 1*

Digital Camera Features

> *Building pictures with pixels*

A digital camera really boils down to an imaging sensor that gathers the light from a scene through a lens, in much the same way that film records a scene in a film camera. The difference is that the digital camera uses electronic devices (photodiodes) that are sensitive to light, in effect gathering light in the form of an electrical charge to ultimately create a digital file that represents the scene before the camera.

Millions of photodiodes on the imaging sensor are used to produce the pixels (individual "dots") in the final image. The sensor itself has dimensions measured in centimeters, and the individual photodiodes are measured in micrometers (one micrometer equals one millionth of a meter). Smaller photodiodes allow for more of them in a given sensor size, translating into more detail in the final image. However, larger photodiodes provide greater tonal range and less noise (random variations in color values among pixels).

> *Building pictures with pixels*

Megapixels	Maximum Recommended Output Size
3	5"x7"
4	8"x10"
6	13"x19"
8	16"x24"
10 or more	20"x30"

It is very difficult to make a choice about which digital camera to buy based on specifications of the imaging sensor. Besides the fact that these details are often presented in a way that would only make sense to an electrical engineer, you really can't evaluate final image quality based on a list of specifications for the camera or imaging sensor. Instead, it is generally best to read reviews of the various cameras you are considering, and to look for key features that meet your needs.

One of the most important factors to many digital photographers (though certainly not the only consideration) is the number of megapixels (millions of pixels) the imaging sensor captures. The number of pixels in the final image determines a general upper limit of print sizes that would be possible from a particular camera, as shown in the table above.

Shooting formats

Digital cameras offer several options for the type of image file that will be produced when you click the shutter. The default setting for most cameras is to capture in a JPEG format, but that may not be the best choice for your particular needs. Consider the file format that represents the best fit for your particular photographic situation.

JPEG represents a compromise between convenience and image quality. It is convenient because it can be read by virtually any software that supports images and it yields a relatively small file size. These can be significant advantages for photographic situations where you favor convenience over image quality. When shooting in JPEG you can fit more images onto a single digital media card, and less processing is necessary to share the files with others. However, the compression that results in smaller file sizes can also negatively impact the image quality. Most digital cameras produce excellent results with highest quality JPEGs, but be aware that you'll want to be sure to get the image perfect in the camera, as you might not be able to edit or enlarge the images to the extent you could with other shooting formats.

The TIFF format provides excellent image quality because it does not utilize compression the way JPEG images do, but the price is a significantly larger file. TIFF images will therefore require more time to write to your digital media cards, and the larger file sizes will fill those cards quite quickly. While many imaging programs support TIFF files, support isn't universal. In general, I don't recommend using the TIFF shooting format.

More advanced digital cameras offer a RAW shooting format, where the file created by the camera isn't an image at all but rather a data file containing the pixel values recorded by the imaging sensor. This format provides maximum potential quality and flexibility, but at the cost of moderately large files and a more cumbersome workflow. Because RAW files aren't really image files, they need to be processed with RAW conversion software in order to be useful. This adds a step to the digital imaging workflow, but is worth it when image quality is of paramount concern.

The JPEG and TIFF options are available with most digital cameras, while the RAW format is typically only offered in more advanced camera models. As a general guideline, use JPEG capture for snapshots or when you need to be able to capture as many images as possible, and use RAW for those special (or challenging) situations where you are trying to produce the best results possible.

Digital media

> *Film for the digital age*

COURTESY OF ISTOCKPHOTO.COM. PHOTOGRAPHER: LEE PETTET.

Digital cameras still use "film," but it takes the form of a digital media card that stores the image files. There are a variety of media types available (such as CompactFlash, SmartMedia, Memory Stick, and others), but most digital cameras only use a single type. Review the specifications for your camera to determine the type of digital media you'll need. The capacity of the card determines how many pictures you're able to take, but the exact number depends on the camera settings you use, such as image quality and file format.

The best way to figure out how big a card you need is to just see how many pictures you tend to take for a given event or photographic excursion. Virtually all cameras display how many pictures will fit on the current card with the current camera settings, so you can monitor your progress. For most casual photographers, a 128MB or larger card will be more than adequate, offering the equivalent of two or more rolls of film. For more serious photographers, capacities of 1GB or more may be necessary to ensure you always have enough space.

TIP: Be sure to install the card properly to avoid damage to the card or the camera. Of equal importance, don't remove a digital media card from your camera until it has powered off completely. Otherwise, you may lose the important photos you've already captured on that card.

Pack the camera bag

> *Fill your bag with tools to help you take great pictures*

Your digital camera is obviously the primary component to taking great pictures, but other tools and accessories will make that task even easier. To start with, before heading for a photo outing be sure the camera battery is fully charged, or that you have backup batteries. Spare batteries are a great addition to the camera bag, as with typical use you'll usually run out of battery power before you fill your digital media cards.

As you pack your camera into the bag, be sure the lens is clean. If you have additional lenses, make sure those are clean as well, so you don't have to think about it if you need to switch lenses in a hurry. Any camera store will sell cloths and solution for cleaning lenses. Or you can use a microfiber cloth designed for cleaning lenses or eyeglasses.

Be sure the digital media cards you're taking along have been formatted or otherwise cleared of images. Naturally, you'll want to be sure you've downloaded any such images to your computer before you clear off the card. Bring enough cards with enough capacity to get you through the number of pictures you expect to capture.

While it won't exactly fit into your camera bag, another great accessory is a tripod. If you aren't willing or able to lug a full-size tripod on a particular outing, a compact tabletop tripod is a viable alternative.

One of the major benefits of digital photography is the ability to immediately review captured images on the LCD display on the back of the camera. However, if you're outdoors it can be very difficult to see this display. There are several commercial shades that allow you to review the LCD even in bright sunlight. In a pinch, the empty cardboard tube from a roll of paper towels provides a great (and cheap!) accessory for viewing the LCD display in sunlight.

> *Make sure you don't miss that all-important moment*

When the digital camera doesn't take a picture immediately upon your pressing the shutter release, it is easy to miss an important moment.

When you press the shutter-release button, a digital camera needs to do quite a bit of work to actually take the picture. As a result, there is a *shutter lag* that causes a delay between the time you press the button and when the picture is actually taken. The exposure/focus lock feature of most digital cameras helps ensure that you won't miss a shot due to this lag.

> *Make sure you don't miss that all-important moment*

Using the exposure/focus lock feature of your digital camera will help you capture the magic moment for every photo.

Most of the delay time is spent determining proper focus and exposure. You can greatly improve your camera's response by locking in the focus and exposure before taking the picture. To do so, compose the scene in the viewfinder or on the LCD, then press the shutter-release button halfway and hold it there. When the magic moment arrives, press the shutter release the rest of the way to take the picture, and it will be virtually instantaneous. Practice getting a feel for how firmly you need to press the button to lock focus and exposure (most cameras provide a green light and audible alert once focus and exposure have been established) without accidentally taking a picture.

When locking exposure and focus, point the camera toward the subject that is most important in the photo. The camera will emphasize the subject matter in the middle of the frame, setting focus and determining optimal exposure settings for that subject. If the subject is off center, lock exposure and focus by pointing the camera at the subject and pressing the shutter release halfway until the camera indicates a lock, then recompose the scene by pointing the camera in a slightly different direction.

The zoom feature

area of
detail

Zooming out for a wider view allows you to capture the overall scene.

The zoom feature available with most digital cameras allows you to change the composition of a scene with great flexibility. With most cameras you adjust zoom with a button that slides back and forth. Push in one direction (usually to the left) and hold to zoom out, and in the other direction to zoom in. Whether you're using the viewfinder or LCD to compose the scene, you'll see the effect of the change in the zoom setting.

> *Changing your perspective without taking a step*

Zooming in allows you to get a closer look, thus isolating the most important elements of a scene.

The greatest advantage of the zoom control is the ability to get closer to your subjects than you might be able to physically. Whether you want to sneak up on a subject that might move if you approach too closely, or you want to fine-tune the composition for the best aesthetic results, the zoom setting makes it easy to change the image on the fly.

In fact, by using various zoom settings for the same scene, you can create many different images. Zooming out completely will allow you to get an overview of the subject, and zooming in will let you extract various elements from the scene. Explore the zoom range offered by your camera, and you'll find countless pictures within pictures.

The flash

In some situations you simply can't get a good photo without flash.

Most digital cameras include a built-in flash, and many of the more advanced models even support accessory flashes that provide more power and greater adjustment options. Flash makes it possible to capture great images in situations that would otherwise prove impossible (or at least difficult).

The most extreme example of the need for flash photography would be in the dark of night. Flash can certainly save the day here, but keep in mind that the flash is only effective to a certain distance, so anything that isn't reasonably close to the camera may appear pitch black in the final image.

> *Add your own light to many photographic situations*

Flash provides an artificial source of light that allows you to take a photo even when no other light is available.

If you are indoors, chances are you'll want to make use of the flash. While the other lighting may be bright, it probably isn't bright enough. In order to capture an image under relatively low light, the camera needs to extend the length of the exposure. While a tenth of a second may seem like no time at all, even people who are sitting perfectly still will show up slightly blurry in the image with an exposure of that duration. Flash adds light to the scene, allowing the camera to use a fast shutter speed (typically around 1/125 of a second) to ensure a sharp image.

For low-light situations, it makes a lot of sense to use the flash on your digital camera. However, just because there is plenty of light doesn't mean you shouldn't use the flash. In fact, if you are in a situation where you need to take a photo in full sun, turning on the flash will produce a better image because it will add fill light to the dark shadows, resulting in an image with soft light that looks more pleasing and natural. I'll explore these issues in more detail later in this book.

Close focus mode

While most digital cameras can't focus on objects that are within a few feet of the lens, many include a feature allowing them to focus much closer, sometimes to within a few inches of the subject. This setting is often referred to as a *macro* focus mode. If you are attempting to take a photo where the camera is very close to the subject, you may not be able to achieve proper focus. Your camera will most likely give you some indication that it wasn't able to focus, typically with an amber light and audible alert.

Switching to the close focus mode changes the operation of the camera so that it can only focus on close objects. With most cameras this covers a range of a couple of inches to a couple of feet between the subject you're photographing and the lens.

Note that this feature is offered as a Macro mode on some cameras, rather than a specific feature to enable close focus capabilities.

> *Gain flexibility in low-light situations*

Increasing the ISO setting on your camera allows you to take photos in low-light settings such as a museum where flash and tripods are not allowed.

If you've ever used a film camera (and believe me, there are plenty of people using digital cameras who've never touched film), you probably are aware that film is available in various ISO/ASA ratings. The higher the number, the more sensitive the film is to light. Higher sensitivity in turn translates into a better ability to capture images in low light.

Most digital cameras include a feature that allows you to adjust the sensitivity of the camera, providing the option to change the ISO rating for the camera from one shot to the next. This is a huge advantage over film, where you'd need to finish off the roll of film before moving on to a roll with a different rating.

Chances are, at some point you'll find yourself in a situation where you need to increase the ISO setting on your digital camera in order to achieve an adequately fast shutter speed in low-light conditions. We'll discuss the use of this feature later in the book.

One of the biggest advantages of digital photography is the ability to instantly view—and share—your images on the LCD as soon as they're taken.

Sharing the images is easy. Simply select the playback option on your digital camera (typically via a button labeled with the standard triangle "play" icon), and the first image will be displayed. Then use the navigation buttons to move from image to image.

Besides sharing images with others, the image-review capability provides an easy way to see whether you captured the image you intended, and delete any shots you don't want to keep. If you find an image that you don't want to keep, press the delete button (typically labeled with a trash can icon) and acknowledge the confirmation message to delete the image, thus making room for another photo on your digital media card.

With many digital cameras, you can also zoom in or out on your images while viewing them on the LCD using the same buttons you use to zoom in or out when taking a picture. This allows you to get a closer look to confirm sharp focus or other details in an image, such as whether the person in the photo had his eyes open. You can also zoom out to view more than one image at a time with most cameras, though they are then too small for you to make most decisions about which should be deleted.

> *Manual control for variable light situations*

White balance is an issue that didn't affect most photographers using film cameras. Most films are *daylight balanced* and produce relatively consistent color under most lighting conditions. Digital cameras, on the other hand, need to consider the color of light so that they can compensate accordingly. For example, incandescent lights produce a very warm light with a yellow-orange appearance, while many fluorescent lights produce a cooler light with a greenish appearance. Digital cameras attempt to determine the color of the light so that they can automatically correct for it and produce photos without undesirable color casts.

In most situations, the automatic white balance setting on your camera works perfectly well. Digital cameras do an excellent job of determining the best setting, and when using automatic you'll probably never even notice any color issues in your photos.

> *Manual control for variable light situations*

However, in certain situations you may find that the camera has a difficult time figuring out the color of the lighting for a scene, causing colors that don't look right. When that happens, you can choose a specific white balance setting to instruct the camera what the lighting is. The white balance settings are usually accessed from a menu on the LCD, and a range of preset options, such as tungsten, daylight, or flash, are available. Select the option that is closest to the actual lighting conditions, checking the results on the LCD to confirm that you are achieving the best color possible.

Part 2

Shooting Modes

> *Keeping it simple...*

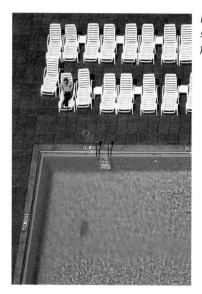

For photos that don't present any special problems, Automatic mode provides a good, easy option.

When you set your camera to the Automatic mode, it will do all the work for you. This is a fantastic way to capture great pictures when you're just getting started and building your confidence using the camera. All you need to do is point your camera at the subject, adjust zoom as desired for the composition, and press the shutter release to take the picture.

In Automatic mode, your camera will automatically determine the optimal exposure settings, will automatically use flash if necessary, and in most cases will produce an excellent photo. In short, if you're at all uncomfortable with the other options provided by your camera, or aren't comfortable with the specific photographic situation, you can use Automatic mode and relax.

> *Keeping it simple...*

The shooting modes offered by most digital cameras are selected with a dial on top of the camera.

The only disadvantage of Automatic mode is the lack of flexibility and control for you, and the chance that the camera might make a bad decision (though this is relatively rare). As you get more comfortable with your camera, start to try out the other shooting modes it offers, as discussed throughout the rest of this section. After all, you won't be wasting any film!

TIP: Most digital cameras offer all of the shooting modes discussed next. However, many cameras will refer to these modes by different names, and some cameras won't offer certain modes at all.

The Program mode

The biggest advantage of Program mode is that it lets you override the flash for tricky shots such as this one. Without the flash, the people in this photo would be too dark to distinguish.

The Program mode can be thought of as an Automatic mode where the camera does a bit more evaluation of the scene to determine the best settings, although the specific implementation of this mode will vary among different cameras. Most digital cameras that offer this setting include a series of preprogrammed lighting conditions along with methods of compensating for those conditions.

The Program mode also tends to offer more control over the various camera features. For example, you may not be able to force the flash to fire while in Automatic mode, while you are able to do so in Program mode.

Program mode is a good choice for tricky lighting situations or for taking photos where you want to exercise a little more control than the Automatic mode offers, without completely giving up the advantages of the automatic features.

The Portrait mode

> *A special shooting mode for the special people in your life*

The Portrait mode is designed to help you produce more pleasing photos of people. To help eliminate distracting backgrounds, when the Portrait mode is chosen the camera will select a wide lens opening (aperture), which minimizes depth of field (the range within the scene that will be captured in sharp focus). This will cause the background behind the person to be blurred to the extent possible, while retaining sharp focus for the person.

Portrait mode will also cause the flash to be set to the red-eye reduction mode if available for your camera (I'll talk more about this option later in the book). This also helps ensure the best portraits possible.

Even if you are only taking casual photos of friends or family, I strongly recommend trying your camera's Portrait mode. It will add a touch of professionalism to every shot, resulting in more pleasing images.

TIP: Because of the relatively small imaging sensors used in many compact digital cameras, and the resulting very small lenses, it can be very difficult to achieve a particularly small depth of field (range of focus). However, using the Portrait mode will help you obtain the narrowest depth of field possible.

The Landscape mode

> *Obtain maximum detail in your scenic photos*

When you want to maintain as much detail in an image as possible, the Landscape mode is your best friend. The Landscape mode will minimize the size of the lens opening (aperture), which will result in maximum depth of field. That means you can maintain crisp focus for all objects in the scene, near and far.

As the name implies, the Landscape mode is most appropriate for vast scenic landscape photos. In such a situation, you typically want to maintain good focus for as much of the scene as possible, so that the final image will retain maximum detail and clarity. While the Landscape mode is designed for landscapes, it can be used in any situation where you want everything in the photo to have good focus.

The Night-Scene mode

> *Digital cameras aren't just for the daylight hours!*

Taking photos at night can challenge your photographic skills, but the Night-Scene mode makes it easy to get great shots. If you use the Automatic mode with a night scene, the flash will be the primary consideration in exposure. The foreground subjects will likely be exposed properly, but the flash can only travel so far, resulting in an excessively dark background (see page 40 for more on using the flash).

The Night-Scene mode combines an exposure that is appropriate for the ambient lighting conditions in the background (which would normally render the foreground subjects as too dark) with the use of flash for proper lighting of the foreground subjects. The result is an image with well-lit foreground subjects but attractive lighting in the background. It is an excellent mode to use in a relatively dark environment, such as a romantic restaurant, where you want to capture the mood of the available light while still producing a proper exposure for the foreground subjects. This gives you the best of both worlds, and can help you obtain memorable images of friends and family while capturing the ambiance of the location.

> *Freeze the action of fast-moving subjects*

When you are photographing fast-moving subjects, getting the best shot normally requires the use of a shutter speed fast enough to freeze the action and render a sharp image. The Sports mode accomplishes this for you automatically. When you use this mode, the camera will attempt to achieve a fast shutter speed to freeze the action.

In regard to fast-moving subjects, you're not limited to cars, airplanes, or speedboats. Anytime you want to freeze the action, even if it isn't lightning fast, the Sports mode will make it easy. Be sure to follow the subject with the camera as you take the picture to ensure that it remains in the frame.

TIP: Freezing the action will result in an image that doesn't express the dynamic nature of the subject. In some cases, you may want to show the sense of motion by using a slower shutter speed, as discussed on the next page.

The Long-Exposure mode

> *Create a mystical or dynamic mood with long-duration exposures*

M ost of the time you want to maintain sharp focus and fine detail in your photos. However, allowing a long-exposure blur in your images helps share the mystical or dynamic quality of the subject, and can be a wonderful way to create a unique interpretation of the scene.

In this shooting mode, the camera attempts to obtain as long an exposure as possible. If the lighting is very bright, this may still result in an exposure lasting only a fraction of a second, but under lower light levels you may have an exposure of several seconds. Regardless, the camera will produce an image with as much motion as possible when using this mode.

There are two ways to approach this type of photo. The first is to place the camera on a stable surface, such as a tripod or table top, so that you can capture a moving subject while maintaining good sharpness for the rest of the scene. For example, you can place the camera on a rock near a stream and capture a long exposure of the flowing water, producing an image with beautiful silky streaks of water. The other approach is to move the camera (called *panning*) along with the subject. If you keep the camera and subject synchronized, the result can be a sharp subject with a blurred background, providing a strong sense of motion.

The Aperture-Priority mode

> *Control the depth of field in your photos*

Use the Aperture-Priority mode to control the depth of field in your photos while letting the camera control proper exposure.

Earlier I talked about the Portrait mode, which is designed to produce images with minimum depth of field (such as the one above), and the Landscape mode, which is designed to produce images with maximum depth of field (such as the one on the next page). This provides you with the two extremes, but as you progress with your photography you'll likely find yourself wanting to exercise greater control over your images. The Aperture-Priority mode allows you to control the depth of field while the camera ensures proper exposure by automatically adjusting the shutter speed.

Specifically, the Aperture-Priority mode allows you to control the size of the lens aperture, which in turn controls the depth of field in your image. However, you should simply think of it as a shooting mode where the priority is determining how much depth of field the image will exhibit.

TIP: The Aperture-Priority mode is often abbreviated *Av* for *Aperture value*, since it controls the size of the lens aperture used during exposure.

TIP: As you get more comfortable using your digital camera, you'll probably find that the Aperture-Priority mode gives you the most artistic control over the image, and you will want to use it more frequently.

> *Control the depth of field in your photos*

A larger, f-stop number creates a wider depth of field, meaning that more objects in the photo are in focus.

Once you've selected the Aperture-Priority mode, you'll need to determine the aperture setting, which in turn will establish depth of field. The aperture itself is established using a setting known as an f-stop, which measures the relationship between lens focal length and the size of the lens aperture. A smaller number (such as f/2.8) represents a larger aperture opening and a narrow depth of field, while a larger number (such as f/8) represents a smaller aperture and wider depth of field.

To adjust the actual aperture setting, you'll typically need to use a "rocker" switch that can be pressed in either direction, or a set of buttons used to increase or decrease the setting. Most digital cameras include the ability to preview the effect of various settings on the LCD display before capture.

The best way to gain an understanding of the effect of various settings in Aperture-Priority mode is to take some test photos. Find a scene that contains near and distant objects, and set your focus on a subject near the lens. Take the same photo with various aperture settings with the camera set to Aperture-Priority mode, and then compare the results of the series of images. This will give you a greater understanding of the effect of each aperture setting on the depth of field of the image, so you're better able to choose an appropriate setting for each photographic situation.

The Shutter-Priority mode

> *Control the exposure time for your photos*

As you take more pictures with your digital camera and gain more familiarity with the apertures and shutter speeds being used to obtain an appropriate exposure, you'll also start to get more familiar with the effect that various shutter-speed settings have on your images. The Shutter (or Time) Priority mode allows you to set a specific shutter speed, and the camera will use an aperture setting that allows you to achieve an appropriate exposure. The Shutter-Priority mode is generally used when you want to obtain a particularly slow or particularly fast shutter speed.

Slow shutter speeds (long exposure times) can be helpful when you want to maintain a dynamic quality in an image and have become familiar (either by experience or experimentation) with the various shutter speeds that will produce the effect you're looking for. For example, flowing water produces a silky effect when captured at shutter speeds of around one-quarter second (see above image). You can also produce dramatic images of people in motion by using shutter speeds of around a tenth of a second.

TIP: The Shutter-Priority mode is often abbreviated *Tv* for *Time value*, since it controls the amount of time the shutter will remain open during exposure. However, most photographers refer to it as Shutter-Priority mode.

> *Control the exposure time for your photos*

Fast shutter speeds (short exposure times) can be helpful when you want to create a freeze frame effect where moving subjects are frozen in time with no visible motion in the image (see above image). For most subjects, such as a child riding a bike or baseball player sliding into home plate, a shutter speed of 1/125 of a second or faster should result in an image with no visible motion. For faster subjects, such as moving cars, speeds above 1/500 of a second may be necessary. Whenever possible, try to test out various shutter-speed settings in advance to determine how fast you need to set the shutter speed to get an image with no visible motion.

TIP: Using the Shutter-Priority mode is a bit more risky than using the Aperture-Priority mode, because there is a greater chance you'll select a shutter speed at which an appropriate aperture isn't available to ensure proper exposure. Keep an eye on the exposure whenever using the Shutter-Priority mode, and be aware that some shutter speeds won't be possible under certain lighting conditions.

The Manual mode

> *Take full control over exposure settings*

The "M" in the top right corner of the LCD indicates that the camera is in Manual mode.

When you start to feel that you've truly mastered your camera and the various exposure options, you may be ready to use the Manual mode. With today's digital cameras, you'll most likely find that the other shooting modes will more than meet your needs. However, when you want to exercise absolute control, or when you need to override what the camera thinks is best for a particular subject, Manual mode puts you in full control. You can adjust the aperture to affect depth of field, and shutter speed to affect the length of exposure.

When using the Manual mode, you control both the aperture and shutter speed, so it is your responsibility to establish settings that will result in an appropriate exposure. The aperture and shutter-speed settings are typically adjusted using two different controls on your camera. An exposure meter should be visible either in the viewfinder or on the LCD (or both) that shows you when your settings will result in a properly exposed image based on the camera's meter.

> *Take full control over exposure settings*

The Manual mode gives you control over setting the proper exposure when the camera is fooled by lighting conditions.

Besides being a great way to take full control over the exposure settings for a given situation, the Manual mode provides all the power you need to produce a proper exposure when the camera is fooled by the lighting conditions. For example, when the lighting is coming from behind a subject, the camera may tend to underexpose too much in order to compensate for the bright sky, resulting in a too-dark image lacking details. Using the Manual mode, you can compensate for the conditions yourself, finding just the right settings for any situation.

The Manual mode is most certainly an advanced shooting mode, but as you gain confidence with your digital photography, you'll no doubt run into situations where the control it provides is exactly what you need.

TIP: If you're using the Manual mode because the camera is fooled by the lighting conditions, you may not want to trust the meter to determine the best settings. Instead, take some test shots as you vary the settings, until you find the settings that give you exactly what you're looking for.

> *Part 3*

Using Light

Professional outdoor and nature photographers have a reputation for being out in the early morning and late afternoon to get the best light (and taking a nap in between!). We've all experienced the warm glow of sunrise, as well as the colorful display of a sunset. Timing your photos to coincide with this lighting can produce magical results.

The key is the low angle of light present early and late in the day. When the sun is relatively low in the sky, the light comes in contact with more of the atmosphere along the way, dispersing the light to produce warm lighting. This can turn what would be an otherwise ordinary scene into an extraordinary photograph.

Planning can make or break a photo when you're trying to include the warm glow from a low light angle. Make an effort to plan for a low light angle when possible, and take advantage of it whenever you find yourself with camera in hand at the right time.

> *Put the light in the right spot*

Putting the sun in the right place can make a significant difference in the quality of your photos. Of course, since you can't move the sun, you'll have to move yourself and your subjects to put the sun where it will give you the best results.

By positioning your subjects and yourself so that the sun is over your shoulder (not directly behind you), you'll ensure a good angle for the light to illuminate your subject. With the sun directly behind you, the subject will be front-lit and will have a flat appearance in the final photo (see the image on the left). With the sun behind the subject, the backlighting creates a photographic challenge (though it can be used for artistic effect when done well).

When the sun is over your shoulder, it casts light across the surface of your subject, creating better depth and texture, with a more pleasing natural lighting (see the image on the right).

If it isn't possible to change the position of your subject, and you can't change your position relative to the subject because of other considerations, you might consider trying to photograph the subject at a different time of day to take advantage of a better light angle.

Sometimes even changing the angle of the light won't produce a pleasing photo. When the light is bright and overhead, it can be virtually impossible to capture a flattering photo of friends and family (see the image on the left). Such lighting can produce harsh shadows and extreme contrast, which can be particularly problematic when photographing people.

The solution to harsh lighting is to find a way to place the subjects in shade (see the image on the right). When photographing people, this can be a simple matter of having them move to a different location, such as under a tree or along the side of a building. You can even create your own shade by holding up an object such as an umbrella to block the light from the main subject of your photo.

Using a backlight

> *Add a sense of drama to your images*

I t is usually best to avoid backlighting of your photographic subject, but sometimes you'll want to put this dramatic effect to use in your photos. You can use this method to create a silhouette of a subject when you are trying to capture a mood or in conjunction with fill flash to make the most of a challenging lighting situation.

To produce a good backlit photo, you'll need to position the subject between you and the light source. For outdoor photos you don't necessarily need to have the sun in the frame behind the subject, as long as the sky is bright enough to overpower the foreground. To obtain an exposure that will render the background properly with the foreground as dark as possible, point your camera at the background and press the shutter release button halfway to lock the exposure on that brighter area of the frame. Then recompose the scene to include your main subject, and press the shutter release the rest of the way.

If you want to maintain a proper exposure of the backlit area while still being able to see the foreground subject, activate the flash on your camera but still set exposure based on the background. This is an excellent way to photograph a subject in front of a sunset, for example, when you would normally end up with a photo in which the foreground was properly exposed but the background was far too bright.

Practice achieving proper exposure with backlighting and you can produce dramatic results from what might otherwise be a challenging photographic situation.

Using flash

> *Add light to the scene for better images*

For straight indoor shots, use the flash.

Mother Nature doesn't always cooperate when it comes to having enough light for a great picture. The simple fact is you need a certain amount of light to be able to use a fast enough shutter speed to get a photo without any blur. When photographing indoors, you'll find that existing artificial light almost never provides as much light as you need. Fortunately, the flash on your digital camera provides a way to get those low-light shots that would otherwise be impossible.

In many of the shooting modes, the flash will fire automatically when needed. If it doesn't fire automatically, turn the flash on so that it will fire even when the camera doesn't think it is necessary.

Keep in mind that the light from the flash on your digital camera can only travel a certain distance. If you are too far from the subject, the light won't be able to illuminate it properly. Also, keep in mind that this same effect will cause the background to be extremely dark in many situations when using flash. You may be able to overcome this problem by using the Night-Scene mode (see page 25).

TIP: Don't move in too close when using flash on your digital camera. Many compact digital cameras will produce images that are far too bright if the flash is used too close. To avoid this, back away from the subject and zoom in to recompose, producing the same image from a greater distance and helping to ensure proper flash exposure.

Using red-eye reduction

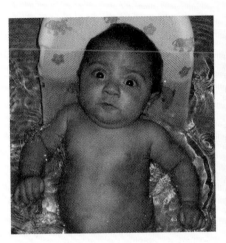 

Y ou've no doubt seen plenty of pictures of people with a red glow in their eyes, referred to (appropriately enough) as *red-eye*. This is caused when the light from the camera's flash bounces off the retina at the back of the subject's eye, directly into the lens. The blood vessels at the back of the eye are what cause the light to be red, and the result is not something we generally consider appealing (see the image on the left).

Most digital cameras include a red-eye reduction mode for the flash that will help minimize red-eye. This feature operates by firing a pre-flash (either as a single light or many small bursts) that causes the subject's pupils to contract. The smaller opening won't let in as much light into the eyes and will lessen the chances of red-eye in the photo (see the image on the right).

The Portrait mode (see page 23) will usually activate the red-eye reduction flash mode automatically, so it is a good idea to simply use this shooting mode whenever photographing people. However, you can also use red-eye reduction flash in other modes by manually setting the flash mode. This is usually accomplished by pressing the flash button on your camera until the red-eye mode is indicated on the LCD.

> *Soften up harsh lighting and enhance detail*

Fill flash is handy for lighting up shadows, such as those created by the deep creases in this flag.

Fill flash is typically defined as the use of a reduced power for the flash so that it only fills in shadows rather than serving as a primary light source. The result is an image with softer contrast, similar to moving the subject into the shade, but possibly more practical depending on the particular situation. In addition to producing more even lighting, fill flash can bring out detail in shadow areas that would have otherwise been hidden.

Most compact digital cameras don't provide the option to reduce the strength of the flash. However, if there is adequate ambient light, the existing light will be brighter than what the flash could have provided. The exposure will therefore be a normal exposure as though no flash were used, but the flash will still reduce contrast and bring out shadow detail.

Whenever you find yourself photographing under strong lighting and you aren't able to move the subject into shade, you don't want to use the "automatic" option for the flash. Under these circumstances, the camera will assume there is adequate light and won't fire the flash. Instead, select the "on" option for your flash to force it to fire. By adding flash even when you don't need it, you'll produce images with softer lighting and greater detail.

TIP: Many digital cameras will only allow you to force the flash to fire in certain shooting modes, so you may need to select one of those modes when using fill flash.

> *Part 4*

Professional
Tips

> *Stay steady for better pictures*

No matter how good you are at holding perfectly still while taking a photo, you'll obtain better images by using a tripod. By placing the camera on a sturdy tripod, you'll be providing a steady platform that will improve the sharpness of your photos.

Virtually all digital cameras include a standard tripod mount on the bottom. Many tripods will mount directly to the camera using a standard screw, while others provide a plate that screws onto the bottom of the camera and then attaches to the tripod.

Naturally, when out taking casual photos, the idea of a big tripod isn't exactly appealing. The perfect compromise is a small travel tripod, often promoted as a "table-top" tripod. This compact tripod is easy to carry in a camera bag or small backpack, while still providing a steady platform. Just be aware that because of its small size, you'll generally need to find something to put such a tripod on top of, such as a table or a wide railing.

As a general rule, if you aren't photographing under full sun, it is best to use a tripod.

TIP: For even better stability, especially when relatively long exposures are required, use the timer feature of your digital camera in conjunction with a tripod. Since the photo isn't taken immediately upon pressing the shutter release when using this option, the camera will be able to "settle down" from your handling and produce a sharper photo.

Minimize the ISO setting

Chances are, at some point you'll find yourself in a situation where you need to increase the ISO setting on your digital camera in order to achieve an adequately fast shutter speed in low-light conditions. Of course, this sort of flexibility comes at a price. The imaging sensor in the camera has an established sensitivity to light. The only way to get greater low-light sensitivity is to amplify the signal. Unfortunately, this also results in more noise (random variations in color values among pixels) in the image (see inset photo).

Using the lowest ISO setting will help ensure minimum noise in your photos, so treat the option to increase it as a last resort. Try using flash, or using a setting (such as the Sports mode discussed earlier) to achieve the fastest shutter speed possible under the existing lighting conditions. If you do have to use a higher ISO setting, be sure to set it back to the minimum value when you're done so that you don't introduce noise into images where you don't really need the higher sensitivity.

Use the histogram chart

> *Find out how good your exposures really are*

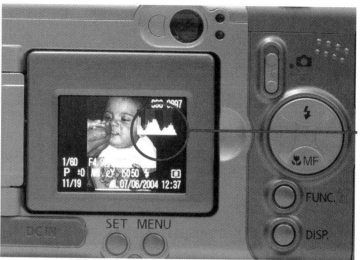

histogram

Looking at the LCD on your digital camera isn't a perfectly reliable way to evaluate proper exposure in your photos. To reliably evaluate the exposure for an image, use the histogram display. A histogram is a chart that shows the brightness values contained within an image. Dark values are represented on the left, and bright values on the right. The height of the histogram display indicates how much of the image contains the values indicated.

The overall shape of the histogram chart is merely an indication of the overall distribution of brightness values within the image. What you want to look for is a histogram that is "cut off" at either end of the scale. Under ideal circumstances, the histogram will resemble a range of mountains that begins and ends within the width of the histogram chart. If the display is abruptly cut off on the left, shadow detail has been lost. If it is cut off on the right, highlight detail has been lost.

I recommend reviewing the histogram anytime you're unsure about the lighting conditions. You can then adjust your camera's exposure settings to achieve a better exposure, resulting in a better histogram.

Optimize the exposure

> *Don't trust your camera completely*

If you're going to be working on your images with photo-editing software, you can help ensure minimum noise and maximum detail by optimizing the exposure for a digital capture.

Because of the way the imaging sensor records image data, you can actually retain more detail by producing an exposure that is as bright as possible without blowing out highlight detail. This will maximize the information within the image. It will also result in less noise because the signal is maximized.

To achieve an optimized exposure, you'll need to evaluate your results with a "normal" exposure, reviewing the histogram to see if it is possible to brighten the exposure without losing highlight detail. If so, either use the Manual mode or an exposure compensation setting (if available) to increase the exposure based on the histogram evaluation. Through trial and error, you'll be able to produce an optimized exposure. With experience, you'll be able to anticipate the exposure compensation required to get the best results under various circumstances.

Keep in mind that when you use this method, you will need to adjust the image using photo-editing software to get the best final image. Out of the camera the image will be too bright, but it will contain maximum detail and minimum noise, which can improve overall image quality.

Simplify the composition

> *Avoid clutter and distractions in your images*

The image on the left is cluttered; the image on the right is much cleaner and yet still portrays the feeling of being in a harbor.

One of the main reasons we take pictures is to tell a story. When we're telling a story with a photo, there is often a tendency to try to tell as much in one photo as possible. In fact, we're often afraid of leaving out an important detail, so we'll back up or zoom out to include everything we feel is important to the subject being photographed.

Unfortunately, this can often produce exactly the opposite of the intended effect. When we include too much in the photo, the viewer doesn't really know what is important, and the result can look cluttered. Instead, try to concentrate on the most important aspects of the subject. What is it you really want the viewer to get from the image? What story are you trying to tell? Make an effort to distill the scene to the most basic elements that make it what it is, and you'll produce much better photos.

Whenever possible, try to concentrate on not including too much in the scene, keeping the composition simple. You'll find that the images look much more professional and do a much better job of telling the story you intended.

> *Show a unique perspective*

Sometimes all it takes to make a great photo is a unique way of looking at the subject. We tend to take pictures that capture the world from the same general angles. Finding a new way to look at the subject provides a way to share the same scene in a new and exciting way that is more likely to captivate the viewer.

As you're photographing a subject, think of all the different ways you could look at it. Move your camera above the subject and look down upon it. Get down on the ground and photograph from below. Experiment with a closer look and a more distant look. Try putting your camera right up to the edge of a subject. Go behind a subject you'd normally only photograph from the front. In short, try to stretch the limits of what is possible, and find new ways to present the same subject in a way that will attract interest.

Zoom with your feet

The excellent zooming capability offered by many of today's digital cameras makes it far too easy to be lazy. The zoom feature is often used to the limit, with photographers wishing they could get just a little bit closer. Of course, in many of those situations it is altogether possible to get closer simply by taking a few steps. Doing so may help you get the best photo possible, rather than settling for what was possible within the limits of your camera's zoom capability.

Whenever possible, I recommend getting close enough to your subject that you can obtain a good photo without changing the zoom from the standard setting. Then use the zoom setting to fine-tune the composition for the best results. This will allow you to use the zoom for an artistic adjustment to the photo, rather than stretching the limits of zoom to get a mediocre shot.

Avoid the digital zoom

> *Maintain optimal quality by avoiding digital zoom*

Most digital cameras include a zoom feature, and many of those also offer a digital zoom to extend the reach of the lens. Don't fall prey to the marketing hype of digital zoom; avoid using it at all costs. While digital zoom will help you fill the frame with the primary subject of your photo, it can also dramatically degrade the quality of the image (see inset image).

When a lens zooms, internal elements provide a genuine magnification factor that results in a closer look at the subject without reducing image quality. Digital zoom doesn't actually magnify the subject. Instead, it crops out a smaller portion of the image and then digitally enlarges it. Some cameras do a reasonably good job of enlarging the image with digital zoom, but most don't. In most cases, you'll obtain much better image quality by zooming only to the optical limits of the lens, and then cropping and enlarging the image later with your photo-editing software.

If your camera includes an option to disable digital zoom, I recommend using this setting to be sure you won't inadvertently activate digital zoom when you are focused on getting a closer look at your subject.

Use natural light

Often natural lighting can produce a warmer, more pleasing effect (left) than can flash lighting (right).

While flash can save the day in many photographic situations where there simply isn't enough natural light to produce a good photo, it may be best to turn it off in some situations. As its name implies, natural light will have a much more natural quality, rather than the sometimes artificial appearance of flash lighting. This is because the flash always has a nearly white appearance, while natural light can provide a warm glow for your images.

Whenever you are enticed by the beautiful cast of a natural light source, or even the not-so-natural but warm glow of artificial lighting, try to obtain a good exposure without the use of flash. This may require that you use a tripod or otherwise stabilize the camera, but the result will be an image that will capture the warmth of the natural light that inspired you to take the picture.

Experiment!

This book has provided you with information on getting the best photos from your digital camera, including some tips on producing professional results. Beyond the information provided here, I strongly recommend that you experiment. Digital cameras provide freedom from that nagging feeling that you're wasting film. They also allow instant feedback, so you can see what's working and what isn't.

Use these tremendous advantages to your benefit, and try new things whenever possible. Think about what you want to say about a particular subject as you're photographing it. What type of photo would best convey the important aspects of that subject? What effect might help the viewer better understand what it was like to be there, experiencing the scene you have photographed?

Always try new things with your digital camera. If an idea enters your mind, give it a shot! If you don't like the results, you can always delete the image. But if you don't try, you'll never know what could have been. Use the tips in this book as a starting point, but then practice, play, and experiment to create photos with your own brand of creativity to share with others.

Index

Index

About the author

A lifetime of working with computers and a love of photography combine as the perfect passion for Tim Grey. He loves learning as much as he possibly can about digital imaging, and he loves sharing that information even more. He does so through his writing and speaking appearances.

Tim's articles have been published in *Outdoor Photographer, PC Photo*, and *Digital Photo Pro* magazines, among others. He is the author of *Color Confidence: The Digital Photographer's Guide to Color Management* (Sybex, 2004), and is co-author of *Real World Digital Photography, 2nd Edition* (Peachpit Press, 2003) and *Photo Finish: The Digital Photographer's Guide to Printing, Showing, and Selling Images* (Sybex, 2004). He teaches courses at the Lepp Institute of Digital Imaging (www.leppinstitute.com), and he lectures and appears at various other venues.

Tim also publishes a regular "Digital Darkroom Questions" email list where he answers questions related to digital imaging for photographers. To add your email address to the list, visit www.timgrey.com.